VEIL OF BLOOD

Rachel McLean writes thrillers that make your pulse race and your brain tick. A proud indie author who manages her own publishing company, she has sold millions of copies digitally and hundreds of thousands in print, regularly topping the bestseller lists. She is the author of the Dorset Crime novels and five spin-off crime series, with beloved characters appearing in multiple series. In 2021, she won the Kindle Storyteller Award with *The Corfe Castle Murders*. She divides her time between Birmingham and Dorset and lives with her wife, three children and two cats Cagney and Lacey.

ALSO BY RACHEL MCLEAN

RACHEL McLEAN

A
MADRID
CRIME THRILLER

VEIL
OF
BLOOD

ROSCOE & McBRIDE

ACKROYD
PUBLISHING

Ackroyd Publishing

ackroydpublishing.com

Printed and bound in the UK by CPI Group (Uk) Ltd, Croydon CR0 4YY

CHAPTER ONE

Dr Petra McBride sank into the armchair, her feet finally free from the torture of her usual four-inch heels. She massaged them and winced at the tender spots. At least the hotel robe was soft against her skin, a small comfort after a long and difficult day. She'd tried the hotel slippers, and they were like sandpaper.

She glanced towards the bathroom. The tub was filling, steam escaping into the bedroom. A bath would help. She needed to unwind, clear her head.

She yawned and blinked at the phone on her bedside table. *Hungry*. She picked it up, hit the button.

"Hola, room service," came the voice on the other end.

"Yes, I'd like to order, please." No point even attempting Spanish; pretty much every person in Spain spoke better English than she did Spanish. Everyone in the courtroom had, even the defendant. "The grilled salmon, and a glass of red wine. Rioja, if you have it."

"Of course, señora. Anything else?"

"That'll be all, thanks."

She hung up, stood, and stretched. Her feet protested as she walked towards the bathroom. She peered at herself in the mirror, rubbing at a smudge of mascara under her eye.

Her sponge bag. She'd taken it into the bedroom this morning when she'd been preparing for court. She left the bathroom, inhaling the perfumed steam as she went.

The TV was on, the volume low. She'd turned it on when she'd got in half an hour ago, for company, and hadn't bothered turning it off.

A news channel: Petra was a news junkie, even if she couldn't understand a word. She caught snippets of Spanish, her grasp of the language shaky at best. But the images were clear.

A man, in handcuffs, being led out of a courtroom. The headline at the bottom of the screen: "*Fuga en los juzgados de Madrid.*"

Even Petra could figure out what that meant.

Escape at the Madrid courts.

She stepped closer, her eyes narrowing. The man on the screen...

Petra put a hand on her stomach. She groaned.

The footage changed. Chaos outside the courthouse. Police were everywhere, sirens, people shouting. That man again, now somehow free of his cuffs. Flailing at a guard, tripping, then getting up again. Running.

She put her hand to her mouth and let out a guttural sound.

"Aw, shit."

She sank onto the bed, her heart pounding. Just hours ago, she'd felt his eyes boring into hers as she gave her evidence. She'd ignored them as best she could, but she could almost read his mind as he listened to her.

So what? Petra was a forensic psychologist whose job it was to understand the nature of crimes so their perpetrators could be tracked down and brought to justice. Pissing off criminals wasn't exactly new territory for her. It was just one of the perks of the job.

But how had he got away?

The bath was still running. Petra forced herself to her feet and hurried to turn off the tap. The room went quiet.

She returned to the bedroom, picked up the remote and turned up the volume. The news anchor was speaking rapidly, the words coming much too fast for her to follow.

But she didn't need to understand the language. She knew who the man was. And she knew what he was capable of.

Her phone buzzed again. She ignored it, her gaze fixed on the screen.

This couldn't be happening.

The room suddenly felt colder, the robe doing little to warm her. She wrapped it tighter around herself, her mind racing.

She needed to know more. Would she be needed?

Most importantly, what would he do next?

CHAPTER TWO

PETRA LEANED FORWARD, eyes fixed on the TV. The footage was from moments earlier. It was shaky, captured by a bystander's phone. Luis Morales, his face twisted with rage, shoved his way through the courthouse doors.

She turned up the volume.

Spanish. It didn't help.

She fumbled with the remote until she found English language subtitles.

"...escaped custody during a court appearance in Madrid earlier today. Luis Morales, convicted of a double murder, is considered extremely dangerous."

The camera panned to the chaos outside Madrid's Audiencia Nacional, the modern court building. Police officers scrambled, shouting in Spanish. Morales moved with purpose, his eyes scanning the crowd.

Petra's stomach tightened. She knew that look. It was the same way he'd looked at her.

Then she spotted Susannah Roscoe, the agent from Interpol who'd hired her to assist with the case. Susannah was in the thick of it. She was heading straight for Morales, her course clear amid the chaos, trying to block his path.

Petra's breath caught as Morales lunged at the agent. The camera didn't capture the impact, but Petra saw Susannah stagger, clutching her side.

"...police and Interpol agents attempted to stop the fugitive. Officers were injured, although details have not been yet provided."

Petra's hands clenched into fists. She'd warned them: Morales wasn't just a killer, he was a predator. And now he was on the loose.

Her phone buzzed. She glanced at it. Not Susannah. Of course not. She ignored it.

The footage looped back to Morales's escape. Petra watched Susannah's face, her determination. She felt a moment of pride. She'd done three jobs for Susannah, all of them freelance. This one had been the most straightforward; Luis Morales wasn't hard to understand.

But now...

She felt a surge of anger. This was her fault. She'd certified that Morales was fit to stand trial. She'd put him in that courtroom.

But what else could she have done? Without her testimony, he'd have walked free or found himself in a low-security facility. And he belonged in jail.

The news anchor's voice droned on. "Authorities are urging the public to remain vigilant. Morales is believed to have connections within organised crime networks."

Petra shook her head. *Wrong.* Morales didn't need connections. He was a force of nature.

The footage cut to a press conference, hastily organised, just yards from where the incident had taken place. A

Spanish police official spoke, flanked by grim-faced officers. All of these people would have been there, at the time. All of them would have seen Morales escape.

"We are conducting a city-wide manhunt. Airports are being monitored. We will find him."

Petra sniffed. Morales wouldn't be caught unless he wanted to be.

Her phone buzzed again: a message from Susannah.

This time, she picked it up.

Petra, I'm fine. But please, call me.

Petra exhaled, relief mingling with guilt. She'd underestimated Morales.

She paused the TV, freezing Morales's face on the screen.

Would they need her help?

Only one way to find out.

She dialled.

CHAPTER THREE

SUSANNAH GASPED IN A BREATH, wincing against the pain in her side.

Morales had hit her with some kind of weapon. Not a knife; there was no blood. And not a gun; he'd never have got one of those into the court building. But something heavy, something more than a fist.

She was leaning against the railings outside the court building, surrounded by people she didn't know. Police, court officials, reporters, members of the public. Everybody was shouting.

She put a hand to her side and winced. *Don't do that again.* Plenty of time to inspect the damage later, when things had calmed down.

Right now, she had a job to do.

Find Luis Morales.

Find him, before he hurt more people.

She stumbled back into the court building, pushing past the people streaming out. Someone bashed into her side, and she cried out, then gritted her teeth.

Ignore it. Focus. This was what Susannah did.

At last, she reached the courtroom. There were only a few people still in there: the lawyers, a couple of officials.

She approached Morales's lawyer.

"Señor Rodriguez, is it?"

He frowned, turning towards her. "*Sí.*" He looked her up and down as if wondering whose shoe she'd come in on the bottom of.

"Where is he?" she asked. Even now, in the moment of crisis, she was confident enough in her language skills to ask in Spanish. "Did he tell you where he would go?"

He laughed. "Do you think I am stupid, Miss...?"

"Roscoe." She pulled out her ID. "Agent Susannah Roscoe, from Interpol."

I arrested your disgusting, twisted client, she thought. *It was me who brought him in.*

And now she'd lost him.

"Where would he go, then?" she snapped. "Where does he feel safe? Where is there someone who'd protect him?"

"I am his lawyer," Rodriguez said. "It is my job to defend him, not to know the minutiae of his personal life."

"It's not your job to help him escape custody. If there's evidence you—"

"*Por favor,*" he said. "Please, do not accuse me of crimes for which you have no evidence." He raised his eyebrows, looking over her shoulder. "I suggest you speak to my esteemed friend."

Susannah turned to find the prosecutor behind her, about to place a hand on her shoulder.

Men. All these men. The lawyers, the judge, the officials, the police. The defendant. At least there had been Petra up there on the stand, explaining what kind of man Luis Morales was.

"What?" she snapped. She didn't see how he could help her.

"Don't think about where he feels safe," the prosecutor told her. "That's not what motivates him. Think about who's next."

She frowned.

"Who's next?" she asked.

A nod. "His next victim."

Susannah's breath caught in her throat. "Petra. Shit."

She fumbled for her phone and dialled Petra. But there was no signal this deep inside the building. She left a message, hoping Petra would get it soon.

"Thanks," she said. Phone still in hand, she ran out of the courtroom into the building's foyer.

A signal. Thank God. But before she had the chance to make a call, her phone was ringing.

Her boss at Interpol, Harry Riley. Another man. Dapper and restrained, he was as English as they came. He was based at Interpol's headquarters in Lyon, not with her in Paris.

"Harry," she said. "We've got a situation."

"I know," he barked back. "I'm watching the footage repeated over and over on every news channel there is. What the fuck happened, Susannah?"

"If you're watching it then you probably know as much as I do." The incident was still a blur to Susannah.

She pushed down the pulsing pain in her side. Did she have Advil in her bag? Where was her bag, anyway?

"How did you let him get away?" Harry said. "We all saw how he went for you. You've made Interpol a laughing stock."

Susannah frowned. Where was the *I saw you were hurt?* Where was the *are you alright?* The *do you need to go to a hospital?*

She breathed in, slow and low, then out again. This was Harry. She should be used to it by now.

"It all happened so quickly," she said. "I'm doing what I can to establish where Morales might have gone. I've spoken to his lawyer."

"He won't tell you anything."

"No. And he didn't. But—"

"*Disculpe.* Agent Roscoe?"

She turned to see the prosecutor approaching. She couldn't even remember his name.

"Yes?" She covered her phone with her hand, ignoring Harry's voice.

"We have found something. In the dock."

She frowned. "Sorry?"

"Letters. They have been etched, with a fingernail, I think. In the wood."

"What?" Graffiti, in the defendant's box? How was that relevant?

"The custody officer has inspected it. He does a full inspection every morning. It wasn't there this morning."

"So, Morales did it." Susannah pulled her hand away from the phone. "Harry, I've got to go."

She ran back into the courtroom, not waiting for the lawyer. A middle-aged man wearing a grey uniform was bent beside the stand where Morales had stood, inspecting the wooden bar.

"What does it say?" she snapped.

He straightened, looking confused.

"*Por favor...*" she said.

He looked at the lawyer, who'd followed her back in at a more sedate pace, and now nodded his assent.

Jesus Christ. Just show me.

"Letters," the official said. "Three letters."

"What letters?" She stood next to him and looked down at the wood.

Oh, shit.

Her breath became shallow. She looked up at the men.

"I know where he's going," she said.

She looked back down at the letters, etched roughly into the wood.

M-C-B

McBride.

Luis Morales' next victim would be Petra McBride.

CHAPTER FOUR

Susannah's number rang out. She'd be busy, if she wasn't on her way to hospital.

Pulling the hotel robe tighter around her, Petra pulled out her laptop and placed it on the bed.

She climbed up onto the bed – yes, she was only five feet tall, but it was a monster – and sat on it, her legs drawn up beneath her. She found the footage of Morales' escape and was replaying it.

The scene was too crowded. He'd somehow broken free as he was being escorted from the court building to a waiting security van. Why had they brought him out this way, anyway? Surely there was a back entrance?

Maybe they wanted to make a show of it. To reassure the public that he was under lock and key.

That, she could understand.

She watched as a guard appeared to fall to the ground next to Morales, but from the camera angle, it wasn't clear what had happened.

And then, a multitude of angles. Reporters standing

outside the courtroom, turning at the sound of the doors being hurled open. Shaky mobile phone footage from members of the public. Gunshots.

Gunshots. The police, she hoped. If Luis Morales had a gun...

Petra clutched the collar of her robe. Suddenly, it didn't feel quite so cosy. She watched as Susannah emerged from the court building, running towards Morales. He turned, something indistinct in his hand, and made a swift, sharp movement in her direction.

Susannah's mouth widened. She collapsed to the ground. Petra couldn't hear her cry over the gabbling reporter, but she felt it reverberate through her.

She dialled Susannah's number again. This time, it went to voicemail.

"Susannah, it's Petra. I hope you're OK. I'm going to run through the materials I used to create my profile of Morales. Maybe there's something that will help us identify where he's gone. I'll call if I find anything."

She put her phone in the deep pocket of the robe, anxious to keep it close. She pushed the laptop away – it was currently showing the commotion on the street as Morales disappeared into the traffic – and went over to her work bag, where her case file was. She pulled it out – *bloody hell, it's heavy* – and placed it on the bed.

A knock at the door made her jump. She took a deep breath – *calm down, you daft hen* – and went to the door, tightening the robe's belt.

"Room service," came a voice.

Her salmon and Rioja. Perfect. She was tired from the trial. Some food would give her the energy to think.

She pulled the door open, smiling. A man was outside,

wearing a face mask; the kind people had worn during the Covid pandemic. No trolley, no tray.

"Petra McBride?"

She nodded. "Where's my food?"

"Forget your food." He raised a hand and pushed his palm against her mouth, grabbing her shoulder with the other hand.

Petra tried to shout. She struggled against his weight, her bare feet slipping.

His fingers were digging into her cheek. She squeezed her eyes shut, then opened them again.

Don't let him in.

She raised an elbow and shoved it in his direction, hoping to give him a deep jab to the ribs. But instead, she felt air, and then the sensation of losing her balance.

He grabbed her, pulled her upright.

"Shut up, if you want to live."

Petra yanked her head back. She pushed against his hand with her teeth.

His hand slipped. She yelled.

But it was too late. He was in the room, and he'd already kicked the door shut.

No one could hear her.

CHAPTER FIVE

THE COURT HAD PROVIDED Susannah with a small interview room to use as a temporary office. She wanted to be out there, chasing Morales down. But she could achieve more with a laptop and a phone.

She'd been using the phone to try to reach Petra for the last five minutes. The first time, it had rung out. The next eight times, it went to voicemail.

"Petra, where are you?" she muttered. Petra had finished giving her evidence earlier in the afternoon and had talked about going back to her hotel room for a long hot bath.

But which hotel?

Susannah had multiple feeds open on her screen. Reports from local law enforcement, trying to spot Morales on the street. CCTV from around the court building. News feeds.

All of it useless, she knew. Morales was cleverer than that.

She dialled Petra's number again; again, voicemail. Then

she had a thought. She ran out of the room, making for the front desk.

The lobby of the court building was calmer now. Most of the reporters had left, probably heading for the disused warehouse in Puente de Vallecas where Morales had taken his victims. Or maybe even his home in Retiro.

He wouldn't go there. Yes, he was a showman who enjoyed publicity. But even he wouldn't taunt them to that extent. She'd agreed with local police that a unit should be sent to both addresses, but she didn't think it would bear fruit.

She ran to the front desk. "I need to speak to someone in your admin department. Specifically, about witness expenses."

The receptionist shook her head. "Sorry, señora, but we do all that online."

"But you must have someone who deals with it. A team. Are they based in this building?"

The woman sucked her teeth. "We don't normally let members of the public have direct—"

"*Mierda!* I'm not a member of the public!" Susannah held up her ID, right in front of the receptionist's face. "I'm an Interpol agent, and I believe one of my witnesses is in danger. She'll have claimed expenses for her hotel room. I need to know where that is."

"Why didn't you say?"

Susannah stifled a scream of frustration as the woman picked up the phone on her desk. She gritted her teeth and tapped her foot vigorously.

"OK," the woman said. "I've got Miguel on the line. Which witness is it?"

"Can you pass me the phone, please?"

"I don't think—"

"This is a life-or-death situation."

The receptionist handed over the receiver with a scowl.

"Miguel?" Susannah said.

"Hello? Who is this?"

"My name is Susannah Roscoe. I'm an Interpol agent assigned to the Luis Morales case. I've shown my ID to your colleague. One of my witnesses could be in danger, and we believe Morales could be targeting her at her hotel. The witness's name is Petra McBride. I need to know if she's made a hotel expense claim, and for which hotel."

"That is a lot of information, señora. Please repeat the name of your witness."

Susannah clenched her jaw. Her Spanish was almost flawless, she knew. Slightly accented, yes, but the man would be able to understand her.

"Dr Petra McBride," she said. "A forensic psychologist who gave evidence on the Morales case."

"The Luis Morales case?"

I already said that. "Yes."

"I am so sorry, señora, but I have been locked out of the records for that case. Security protocols, following the incident today."

"Following his *escape*," she said. "And the fact that he's most likely heading to my friend's hotel room now."

"I can assure you, señora," Miguel said, "that the defendant will not have been able to access the records, either. Nor his legal team. This is why—"

"OK, Miguel. I know this isn't your fault. But how do I access the records? I need the name of Dr McBride's hotel, and I need it now."

Morales was clever. His crimes had been planned in

detail. His escape would have been, too, regardless of how spontaneous and chaotic it had looked at the time.

If Luis Morales was looking for Petra, he'd have done the groundwork. An associate would have identified her hotel before the trial started.

"I can speak to my supervisor," Miguel said.

Susannah clapped a hand to her forehead. *Heaven save me from bureaucrats.*

"Yes," she said. "You do that. And tell me the instant you're able to access that file."

CHAPTER SIX

PETRA STEPPED BACK into the room, but he was too fast for her. He tightened his grip over her mouth, shoving fingers between her lips. She pushed against them, her breathing shallow, but he was stronger than she was.

"Be quiet, shrink." He leaned on the door, checking it was closed, then shoved her further into the room.

Petra flung out her hands, trying to grab a door handle, a table, anything she might be able to push back against. If she could find something to take her weight, then maybe she could lift both legs and kick him.

He grabbed both her hands in his. As his hand left her mouth, she screamed. He kicked her shin, wrapped one large hand around her ridiculously small ones, and put the other back on her mouth.

She shook her head, but his grip was too strong. He pushed his weight into her and shoved her towards the bed.

Petra had taken a self-defence class, back when she'd worked at Dundee University. She couldn't remember much of it, but...

She turned, twisting her body so she could lean into him with her hip. She pointed her fingers to narrow her hand, then twisted that, too.

She pushed into him with her hip, bringing her foot up behind his knee to topple him. Simultaneously, she yanked her hand downwards.

But she was too close to the bed; her legs were already against it. Instead of pushing him over, the movement sent her toppling onto it.

She scrambled across it, making for the phone on the bedside table. *Thank God for landlines*. But he yanked at her robe and pulled her backwards. He smacked an elbow into the side of her head.

Petra yelped. The room had blurred, and her legs were jelly. She took deep, quick breaths – one, two, three – to recover herself.

But it was no good. He grabbed her arm, twisting it at an angle that made her cry out. He spun her over and slammed her onto her back. His splayed fingers pushed into her collar-bone and pinned her down.

Petra could hardly breathe. She stared up at the ceiling, refusing to make eye contact with the man. She blinked.

Was she going to die here? He seemed desperate enough.

"What do you want?" she asked, her voice muffled through his fingers.

"*Español*," he said. His voice was sharp. She knew that voice.

"I don't speak Spanish," she grunted back. "*No hablo Español*."

"Stupid Englishwoman." He spat into her face.

"Scottish, I'll have you know," she replied. It came out as garbled nonsense.

He lifted his knee and pushed it into her stomach. Petra squeezed her eyes shut, grimacing at the pain.

Room service. They were bringing her order. If she didn't answer the door, would they let themselves in?

Just hold on till then, she told herself.

She hadn't told Susannah where she was staying, and her conversations with the prosecutor and the investigating judge had been purely professional.

No one knew she was here.

Even if they guessed he would come for her, they didn't know where she was.

So how the hell did he?

"How did you find me?" she mumbled.

He lifted his hand from her mouth. His eyes flashed. "You scream, I hurt you."

She knew his English was better than that. He was an intelligent man, an educated one. He'd planned his crimes in meticulous detail. He'd spent more than a year before his arrest presenting as depressed and delusional to anyone who would pay attention. All so he wouldn't end up in prison.

But Petra had seen through that. And Petra's evidence had convinced the judge that prison was where he belonged.

"I know who you are," she growled. "Take that fucking mask off."

The blue mask, where had he got that?

He yanked the mask off and gave her a broad smile. "Hello, Dr McBride."

Petra tried to ignore the pain. Her stomach, her hand, the side of her head.

"Why are you here?" she said.

Did she want to know the answer?

Luis Morales leaned back, his legs still straddling her.

"You don't need to ask that, do you, Dr McBride?" he said, his English perfect and barely accented. "You already know the answer."

CHAPTER SEVEN

Susannah was trying to distract herself.

She knew that hovering in the lobby, waiting for Miguel to call her back after speaking with his supervisor – who wasn't in the building right now – and accessing Petra's expenses claim, would send her insane with worry and impatience. Not to mention that it would make her extremely unpopular with Lourdes, the woman on reception.

So after providing both Lourdes and Miguel with her mobile number and the location of her makeshift office, she'd gone back there. And continued in her quest to track Morales down.

National police were running traces on CCTV within a one-mile radius, which meant hundreds, if not thousands, of cameras. They had AI-assisted recognition software to help identify his face in the Madrid crowds, but all he had to do was put on a baseball cap and they were screwed. They'd also set up identifiers for his face on the biggest social media platforms, hoping he might appear in the background of a tourist video.

So far, nothing.

Susannah had access to her own systems. While on the phone to Javier Ortega, her Policía Nacional contact in Madrid and the man who'd helped arrest Luis Morales, she'd established a secure internet connection on her laptop and was putting out feelers in the sorts of places traditional law enforcement might not look.

Susannah was a regular visitor to the dark web. She had user accounts on multiple forums, all set up using layers of security deep enough to deter even the most determined hacker.

She scanned the chatter, or what passed for chatter in these dingy online nooks and crannies. There was the usual speculation, those approving and disapproving of Morales' escape and of the crimes that had led to his arrest. There were fanboys, disturbed individuals who seemed to actually admire him. Some of them were on watch lists, being observed by Interpol or by law enforcement in their own countries, where it had been possible to ascertain their location.

Lots of chatter, sure. But nothing concrete. Nobody was revealing anything about how Morales had planned his escape or what he might do next.

Nothing useful, anyway. Nothing beyond speculation and conjecture. One person seemed to have come to the same conclusion she had, without any evidence that they knew of that etching in the courtroom.

Petra. The speculation that Morales might target her had led to a flurry of memes and fantasies, some AI-generated, many obscene.

Sick bastards.

But none of them knew a thing. None of them, it seemed,

were actually acquainted with Morales, no matter how much they might claim to know him in their hearts. And no one was claiming, or even hinting at, involvement in his escape.

Her phone rang and she pounced on it.

"Agent Susannah Roscoe. *Dígame.*" *Speak to me.*

"Agent Roscoe. It is Miguel. From the Audiencia Nacional accounts department."

"Miguel. Please tell me you have good news."

A pause.

"Miguel?"

"Sorry. Yes. I was just conferring with my supervisor."

Dear God. "You've got access to Petra's expenses, right?" She held her breath.

"Yes," he said. "I have an expense claim for the Hilton Doubletree, on Calle de San Agustín."

Susannah felt relief wash over her. "Thank you."

She picked up her phone and dialled her local police contact.

"I need officers at the Doubletree by Hilton now. My witness, Dr Petra McBride, is there. She could be in danger."

CHAPTER EIGHT

PETRA STARED BACK AT MORALES.

You already know the answer.

He was right; she knew why he was here. Knew what kind of man he was.

He'd pushed her into the room, shoved her onto the bed. He'd been here, what, ten minutes now?

Maybe not that long. Maybe longer. It felt like longer.

She knew what kind of man he was. She'd seen the photos of his victims. Even she, an experienced forensic psychologist, had had to turn her face away from some of them.

He was a violent man. A man who didn't hesitate to attack, to hurt, to kill.

But he hadn't hurt her. Not yet. Not properly. A whack in her ribs was nothing, compared to those photos.

She shunted backwards and pulled herself up to a sitting position. He was standing at the end of the bed, a knife in his hand – still in his hand, still unused – staring at her with a look of disgust.

She pushed back a smile. *I know what it is you want, laddie.*

And it wasn't to hurt her. At least, not yet.

Not until...

Her long hair was loose, a lock of it hanging over her eye. She pushed it back. She straightened her back and lifted her chin.

Show him you're not scared. Show him you're prepared to listen.

"How did you get away?" she asked. "From the court building?"

He frowned. "Why should I tell you that?"

He was speaking English. Perfect English.

You're not going to convince me if you carry on like this.

But he wanted to show off. His desire to impress, always there, and always acting against his desire to be seen as mentally incapacitated. As not responsible for his actions.

His eyes widened. He leaned towards her. She could smell sweat and adrenaline.

Don't show your fear. He needs you to be a professional.

"What is it you need from me?" she asked.

Need. Not *want. Want* was risky.

His right eye twitched. "I want you to suffer. I want—"

"Not what you *want*, Luis. What you *need*. You came here because you need something from me."

Her breathing was shallow; her skin covered in goose-bumps. She was sweating in the heavy hotel robe.

Could he see that? Would it help her, or work against her?

"I told you. I want you to—"

She held up a hand. After a moment's hesitation, she

leaned forward, kneeling now. She held his gaze, aware of the knife in his hand but not looking at it.

Where had he got it? An accomplice? Was there someone out there in the hall right now, keeping guard?

She swallowed. *No.* Luis Morales was a lone wolf. All of his crimes had been committed alone. She'd known that from the case files before she'd even known who he was.

He cocked his head. "You think you know what I want, Scottish bitch?" He twitched the knife in his hand.

Ignore it. She forced herself to edge towards him, to get a few centimetres closer.

Jesus Christ, Petra McBride. Are you some kind of idiot?

Men like Luis Morales were men you ran from. Not men you approached. But she was going nowhere. And she had her own weapon.

"I have no idea what you want, Luis. Probably the same things all the rest of us want. Your freedom, for one thing. But that's not what I asked."

He sneered. "What did you ask?"

"I asked you what you need."

He barked out a laugh. "Need. Want, need. *Queiro, nece-sito.* What is the difference?"

But he knew. Something had settled in his eyes. And his English was good enough. She didn't need to attempt the Spanish translation.

You shouldn't have been so intelligent, Sonny-Jim.

"You need out. You need not to go to jail. Wouldn't anyone? You need that a hell of a lot more than you want to hurt me. Am I right?"

"Both. I can do both. I am already free. And you..." He waved the knife in her direction.

Petra forced herself not to flinch.

"No," she said. "You can't. My friend. Agent Roscoe. She'll know you're coming for me. She saw the way you looked at me, when I was giving my evidence. And she knows the power I hold for you."

He turned his head to one side and spat.

"Power? *Coño!* You hold no power, woman. Look at you."

Yes, look at me. Still sitting here, talking to you. Not dead, like your other targets.

"My evidence dictates whether you go to prison. All this" – she gestured around the room – "is designed to show me that you're mad. Not bad."

"What is mad, not bad?"

"Oh, I think you know." She'd used those exact words when prompted by the judge. Morales would have picked up on them, and on the translation in court.

He stood still, staring at her.

So she was right. Of course she was right. She understood the contents of his mind better than he did.

An occupational hazard. One that wasn't entirely pleasant, to put it mildly.

"So how are you going to convince me?" she said.

He frowned. "Convince you?"

"That you're not mentally capable. That you weren't in control of yourself when you committed your crimes. That you shouldn't go to prison."

He wrinkled his nose. Disdain, mixed with consideration. "By hurting you."

"Uh-uh." She shook her head. "If you hurt me, they'll never let me give evidence. I won't be a credible witness. Will I?"

Dear God. Bolster a man's ego, appeal to his intelligence. All to make him think you believe he doesn't have any.

He took another step forward and lowered himself onto the bed, so he was perching on its end. He placed the knife on the sheet, by his leg.

"I talked to the therapist, the one they made me see after my arrest."

Of course you did.

She nodded. She knew what he was going to say next.

"Trauma?" she asked. "In childhood?"

"You knew. And you didn't say a word about it in your evidence." He stood up. "Bitch."

She put up a hand; *calm down.* "I didn't know," she said. "I saw none of your arrest records. All I was working on was the evidence from the crimes you committed. My job is to determine the psychology of a criminal, by looking at his actions."

"At what I did."

"At what you did."

"Not at what was done to me."

Petra licked her lips. "Why don't you tell me about that? Help me understand."

His eyes narrowed. He lowered himself to the bed.

Petra drew the robe tighter around herself.

"OK," he said. "You will understand. I promise you, you will."

She nodded, forcing a smile of understanding.

Susannah, where are you?

CHAPTER NINE

SUSANNAH JUMPED out of the police car and slammed the door. She scanned the street. More cars were already there: blue lights, no sirens. Even the blue lights might be enough to draw Morales' attention, but it was too late to do anything about that now.

She ran into the hotel, pinpointed the reception desk, and sprinted to it. Yanking her ID from the inside pocket of her jacket, she barked at the receptionist.

"My name is Susannah Roscoe. I'm an agent for international police, Interpol. I have a witness staying here who could be in danger. I need her room number."

The receptionist was young, her hair scraped back into a bun.

"Guest whereabouts are confidential. I'd have to—"

Susannah pushed her ID closer to the woman. She turned at the sound of footsteps and was relieved to see three, four, five police officers enter the lobby. Hotel guests stood up from their seats or drew in towards the walls, anxious.

"This is an emergency," Susannah said. "A man escaped custody this afternoon. You might have seen it on the news."

The woman's hand went to a crucifix on a short chain around her neck. "Luis Morales?"

Susannah nodded. "We have reason to believe he's targeting our witness. And she's staying here. So if you'll—"

"*Aqui?* He's in this hotel?" the woman replied. She crossed herself.

"Give me her room number, and we can deal with him."

One of the police officers was approaching the desk. His colleagues were calming the members of the public down, moving them out of the building.

"Quickly, please," Susannah said.

The young woman nodded. "What's her name?"

"Agent Roscoe," said the police officer. "I'm in charge of this location now. *Por favor*, let me and my men handle this."

She raised a finger. *One of your 'men' is a woman*, she stopped herself from saying. "I know Petra. She trusts me."

"She is not the only person at risk."

No, but she's the person most at risk.

Susannah ignored him. She focused on the receptionist.

"Her name's Petra McBride. Can you find her?"

The young woman looked up. She looked like she might cry. "There is no Petra McBride in our system."

Shit. Had she got the wrong hotel?

Then Susannah remembered. Petra used an alias. A figure from Scottish history.

Who?

"Try Mary," Susannah said. "Mary..."

What was the woman's surname? Petra would hardly check into a hotel as Mary, Queen of Scots.

"Mary Stuart?" the receptionist asked.

The policeman leaned across the desk. "You need to lock this building down. Agent Roscoe can't—"

A door opened in the wall behind the desk. A woman in her late fifties, unfeasibly glamorous, emerged.

"Officer," she said. "How can I help you?"

The officer, who still hadn't introduced himself to Susannah, took the newcomer to one side and began speaking in a low voice.

The receptionist leaned over the desk. She beckoned Susannah closer.

"Room 522," she said. "And use the stairs. If the hotel is locked down, the lift will be shut off."

CHAPTER TEN

Morales laughed. "Stupid woman."

Petra felt her mouth twitch.

He shook his head. "I know what you're trying to do. You're stalling me, trying to get me to talk. You want me to prove to you that I'm mentally unhinged."

Petra tried not to listen to how fast her heart was beating.

"All I want to do," she said, "is talk to you. To listen to you. I'm a psychologist. That's my job."

He smirked. "Oh, I know what your job is, Dr Petra McBride." He held out a hand and beckoned. "Give me your phone."

She frowned. "Why?"

"Just give me your phone."

Damn. She'd thought she had the upper hand. But Morales was intelligent.

"OK," she said. "It's in the bathroom."

"Where in the bathroom?"

"On the vanity unit, next to the sink."

His gaze darted to the landline on the bedside table. "You fetch it. I will watch you."

Petra edged her way off the bed. Morales watched her, his features impassive. She tried to keep him in her sight all the way. But when she reached the bathroom door, she had to turn her back on him.

She closed her eyes. *Don't hurt me. I can be useful to you.*

"Don't try anything, shrink. Just grab the phone and give it to me."

Petra reached for the phone, her movements as smooth as she could manage. She turned back to him and held it out.

"Here."

He grabbed it and stuffed it into the back pocket of his trousers with one hand. The other still held the knife.

"Back on the bed," he said.

Petra edged around him towards the bed, careful not to make physical contact. She clambered onto the high bed, pulled her robe tighter, and leaned against the headboard.

She was naked under the robe. She hoped he hadn't worked that out.

"Stay there." He brought out her phone and jabbed at it.

"I can help you," she said.

He looked up from the phone. "I know you can. And that is what you are about to do."

He'd taken photos of his victims. Serene poses, almost beautiful. He'd cleaned them, arranged them. He'd known that he as much time as he wanted, that no one would disturb him.

How long had he been watching those women, to know that?

There had been no such opportunity to watch Petra. She'd only arrived here two days earlier.

"I'm impressed you found me," she said. "I assume you had someone working for you? Did they watch me leave the court building?"

He grunted. "Shut up. Give me the access code for your phone."

Everything in her life was on that phone. But Petra wasn't stupid. He couldn't access case files without going through extra layers of security.

She gave him the code.

"Good," he said. "Sensible move, shrink."

Not a shrink, she wanted to say. Instead, she just nodded.

He jabbed at the phone a few more times then held it up, pointing it at her.

Her legs weakened. *Photos*. He wanted souvenirs.

"What are you doing?" she asked, then cleared her throat. *Don't show him your fear*.

He smiled. "Filming you. You're going to read a statement for me."

CHAPTER ELEVEN

Susannah slammed through the door to the stairwell, blocking out the voices behind her.

Room 522. Only five flights up, hopefully.

She was wrong. The next level was another reception floor, signs to a restaurant and leisure centre.

Keep going. Susannah took the stairs two at a time.

After five more flights, she stopped, standing by the door that would take her out of the stairwell.

She had her gun, and she had the advantage of surprise. Unless Morales had an accomplice watching the hotel, he wouldn't know she was coming.

But if he did...

The blue lights. The officers taking over the lobby. He must have had someone follow Petra, or how would he know where she was?

Damn. He's expecting us.

He knew the police were here. He was expecting an armed raid.

He wasn't expecting a lone female agent. Could she use that?

Her phone buzzed and she grabbed it. An alert on Petra's name. She'd set one up as soon as Petra had agreed to help with the Morales case.

YouTube. A live streaming video, with her name in the title.

Oh, God. Had he killed her? Was he already gloating, publicly? Was he about to kill her, and broadcast it live?

No. Morales was a monster, but he wasn't a terrorist. And he adored attention.

The video screen was black. Susannah put a hand on the door out to the corridor.

She could go out there, stop this before it happened. But if Petra was about to appear live, that would provide information. And if Petra was as smart as Susannah knew her to be...

She opened the door a crack. The corridor was clear. She pulled out earbuds and plunged them into her ears.

The screen changed. Petra, dressed in a hotel robe, her back to a headboard. Her hair was down, her face clean of make-up.

She'd lost her armour. The up-do, the suit, the heels. She looked ten years younger.

Susannah touched her fingertips to the screen. *Be safe, Petra.*

A hand entered the screen from the right. A male hand, by the looks of it. It handed Petra a sheet of paper.

The psychologist took the paper, licked her lips, and began to read.

CHAPTER TWELVE

PETRA SCANNED the sheet of paper Morales had handed her.

It was predictable enough; a retraction of everything she had said about him in court, an assertion that in fact, Morales was driven by mania and psychosis, and that he hadn't been in control of his actions when he'd committed his crimes.

What he didn't seem to realise was that a man who would go to the trouble of escaping from custody, seeking out a witness and forcing her to read these words, was very much in control of his actions.

"Read," he snapped, waving the knife at her.

She sighed. None of this would affect his case. But it would buy her time.

Susannah, where are you?

"Read."

She nodded and looked at the phone. Morales held it in his hand, which...

Was he shaking?

"My name is Dr Petra McBride," she said. "I am a freelance forensic psychologist hired by international law enforcement to give evidence in the trial of Luis Morales."

She glanced over the top of the sheet at Morales. *Really?*

He frowned and gestured with the knife.

"You may have seen me on television," she said. "Arriving at the trial."

Seen me on TV? Was this just a man desperate for his fifteen minutes of fame?

She read the next paragraph to herself. Details of who she was, of why she'd been hired. He'd done his research.

Nobody needed to know all that.

"I am currently with Mr Morales," she said. "He has asked me to make this statement and believes that I can convince you of his psychological challenges."

"No," he hissed. "Not your words. *Read.*" He pushed urgency into the final word.

Fine, she thought. *Pacify him. Buy more time.*

"I was brought into this case because of my experience in helping the police identify and apprehend criminals whose offences have a psychological nature. In Scotland, I helped identify the man now known as the Macbeth killer. In New York, I assisted the police in the identification of the grocery store murderer."

Dear God. Was listing the ridiculous nicknames of the men she'd helped to find supposed to impress the audience?

"Luis Morales is different from those men," she continued, reading. She peered over the top of the paper into the lens, then lifted the paper slightly, drawing attention to it.

In case you hadn't noticed, dear viewer, I am reading this. These are not my words.

She peered into the camera again and raised one eyebrow. *Cynicism.*

"Read," Morales hissed. "Stop stalling."

She looked up at him and nodded, then looked back down at the sheet.

"Luis Morales is not like those men," she said. "The Macbeth killer was an intelligent, analytical criminal. He planned his crimes, picked out his locations, and worked his way into the investigation. At first, I was taken in by him, but then I realised what he was doing, and helped the police apprehend him."

For fuck's sake. Did people really want a potted history of her time working with Police Scotland?

She scanned the paragraph dealing with Todd Nicholson, the so-called grocery store murderer. Just as dull.

"Men like him," she said, "and men like the grocery store killer..." She leaned towards the camera and intensified her gaze. *This is me speaking.* "They are calculated and organised. They know what they are doing, from the initial planning of their crimes to their execution."

She'd lowered the sheet of paper, holding it in shot but away from her line of vision. *I'm not reading this, not now.*

"My job, or a part of it, is to identify if a killer is organised, if he knows what he's doing, or if he's driven by mental illness. I read this from the crimes themselves, not from knowing the criminals or even meeting them, in most cases."

She raised the paper again, holding it out in front of her. She looked down at it and back at the camera. *Reading.*

Morales stepped forward, then stopped when he realised he'd made the camera shake. He bared his teeth at her. *Read.*

Petra nodded, the paper still raised.

"Luis Morales," she said, barely raising her eyes from the paper, "is not like those men." She adjusted her voice to make it more monotonous, like a child reading from a prepared end-of-term speech. "He did not plan his crimes. He did not even know he was going to commit them until moments before he did. He was engulfed by a psychotic rage for which he was not responsible and which he can barely remember. He regrets his actions but cannot be held fully accountable for them."

Morales stood stiffly. He'd made a fatal error: holding the phone in his hand. It meant he couldn't move. It meant he couldn't hurt her.

Not unless he wanted it to be witnessed live. And he knew he'd never be able to simulate psychotic rage for the camera. Not convincingly.

Luis Morales, as Petra had known all along, wasn't stupid.

"Finish it," he growled.

She looked up at him again, nodded, then looked at the camera.

"I'm asking you to trust my professional judgement," she said. "Luis Morales found his way to my hotel room and engaged me in conversation," – *going off script again* – "and was able to convince me that I was wrong in my initial judgement." She raised the paper – *back on script* – "I have seen his behaviour and his actions, including the threats he has made against me, and I now believe he is under the influence of a delusional psychosis. He needs help, not punishment."

She closed her eyes.

Had that been enough? Had she navigated the tightrope that would keep her alive while telling the truth about the man in front of her?

He flung the phone onto the bed, camera pointing towards the ceiling. It was still recording.

"Fucking bitch," he said.

Petra put a hand to her stomach. She felt sick.

"Fucking bitch," he repeated, his voice level. "You stupid, stupid fucking bitch."

CHAPTER THIRTEEN

Susannah crouched on the floor beside the door to Petra's corridor, her phone on her hand.

Petra, you legend.

She was reading the script Morales had given her, but she was doing more than that. She was adding her own words and using her body language to convey her true meaning.

When she spoke his words, she looked down at the paper and spoke in a monotone. It was like watching the world's worst public speaker.

But every now and then, she would let the sheet of paper drop. Or she would use facial expressions: a raised eyebrow, a frown, a concerted stare into the lens.

These were Petra's own words. If they weren't her own words, they were her own meaning.

"I now believe he is under the influence of a delusional psychosis. He needs help, not punishment," Petra said in a monotone.

Petra was telling the world what Luis Morales wanted

people to hear. He'd talked to her. He'd convinced her. He wasn't of sound mind.

And at the very same time, she was saying the exact opposite.

The shot changed, Petra's face replaced with a moving image. A bed, Petra's legs in a hotel robe, and then...

The ceiling?

The camera was lying face-up on the bed.

"Fucking bitch. You stupid, stupid fucking bitch." Morales's voice.

Susannah felt her blood run cold.

The screen went black.

Shit.

Susannah glanced behind her. Four uniformed officers were on the stairs, also watching the broadcast. The man at the front, the inspector, looked at her.

"What now?" she said.

"You know her," he replied in Spanish. "Is she in immediate danger?"

Petra was clever. She could outsmart Morales. But he was violent. Cold-blooded and violent.

"Yes," she replied. "She is."

"Then we go in there. Right now."

No waiting. *Thank God.*

"Good," she said.

"You at the back," he replied.

She nodded. The officers were armed, and this was what they were trained for.

The inspector gave his colleagues a few words of instruction, his voice low and calm. He gave Susannah a nod.

She stood back. The four officers – three men, and one woman who raised an eyebrow at Susannah when she passed

– moved into the corridor. Their movements were smooth, fast and quiet. One of the men hung back to position himself in front of the doorway. The others advanced.

When they were two doors away, the door to Petra's room opened.

Susannah was behind the door to the stairs, watching through a crack she held it open by. She pulled back, breath catching in her throat.

The inspector raised a hand. His colleagues stopped moving. Like a single creature made of separate parts, they pulled into various doorways.

Susannah held her breath.

A figure emerged from the open doorway. A short woman with long dark hair, dressed in a hotel robe and hotel slippers.

Petra.

Susannah rocked forward, one foot through the doorway.

No. It wasn't her job to rescue her friend. She realised that over the three cases she'd worked with Petra, two of them more than four years ago, that was how she'd come to think of her.

She waited. Would Morales be behind her? Was he restraining her? Pushing her out, his knife to her throat?

No. Petra was alone.

The female officer stepped forward and held out a hand. Petra reached for it, then fell forward into the woman's arms.

Susannah's chest felt tight.

I'm right here, she thought. She wanted to be out there, giving Petra that hug. Telling her she was safe.

After a few moments, Petra straightened up. She scanned the corridor.

"Where is she?"

"Where is who?" asked the female officer.

Petra looked between the officers. "Susannah. Agent Roscoe of Interpol."

The inspector looked back towards the door. There was still no sign of Morales.

Where the hell was he? Was this a trap?

Petra hurried past the police officers, towards Susannah. She allowed Susannah to fold her in a hug.

"You found me," she said. "How did you find me?"

"Your expenses claim," Susannah replied.

A smile spread across Petra's face. "Well done. Well done. Bloody brilliant."

"What about Morales?" Susannah asked. "Is he still in there?"

Petra raised an eyebrow. "Where else would he be?" She squeezed Susannah's hand. "He's not going to give you any trouble. He knows the jig's up."

"The jig's up?"

"I tried to be subtle, but he saw through me. He knows that statement won't work. And he can't retract it... or make me retract it."

Petra glanced back. The officers had disappeared. Susannah could hear muffled voices.

"He'll cooperate," Petra said. "He knows it's his only option."

CHAPTER FOURTEEN

SUSANNAH LOOKED up as Petra entered the hotel bar. In front of her were four glasses: two of water, two of wine.

"No whisky?" Petra said as she approached the table. Susannah was watching her with a look that said she wasn't quite sure whether to smile.

"Sorry. I'll reorder."

Petra put a hand on Susannah's arm. "Wine is fine. And the water. I need that, too." She grabbed a glass of water, downed it and then picked up her wine glass and took a generous swig.

Susannah watched in silence, her eyes full of concern.

"Oh, that's better," Petra said. Her heart was still racing. Sitting on that bed, thinking as fast as she could while she spoke into the camera. She'd tried her best to appear calm, but she'd certainly not felt it.

"How are you?" Susannah asked. Her fingers were travelling up and down the stem of her glass, but she wasn't drinking.

"I'll be OK," Petra replied.

"You aren't yet, though."

Petra felt a muscle in her forehead twitch. She took another swig. The glass was almost empty. Susannah topped it up.

"I shouldn't," Petra said.

"If it helps..."

"Is this what you do with all your witnesses? Calm them with alcohol?" She picked up the bottle. It was Spanish, of course: Verdejo. Good, as far as she could tell. But she was hardly an aficionado.

Susannah smiled. "We reserve the gold service for our most valued witnesses."

"We? I don't see anyone else from Interpol here."

Susannah scanned the bar. "That man over there, with the handkerchief in his top pocket. He's undercover."

Petra laughed. "You're Interpol, not MI6. But thanks."

Susannah sipped her wine. "What for?"

Petra held out her free hand. She was wearing her favourite blouse, shades of pink and red. Her hair was still down, but it had finally been washed and blow-dried.

"See?" she said, looking at the hand.

Susannah followed her gaze. "What am I looking at?"

"You clearly didn't notice, back up there in the corridor. My hands were shaking like bloody castanets. You made me relax."

"Glad to have helped." Susannah raised her glass and Petra clinked it.

It was fun, this act. Calm, professional, mildly flirtatious. But it was an act. Petra was a psychologist, and she knew she couldn't just shake off what had happened this afternoon.

"I'm sorry about what happened," Susannah said. "Morales should never have been able to escape like that."

"No," Petra agreed. "Who was it that fucked up?" She touched Susannah's hand. "I'm not suggesting it was you."

"Oh, it probably was me, to some extent."

"It wasn't." Petra lowered her voice. "Your job was to apprehend him. To build a case, to bring in witnesses. Keeping him in custody was the job of... who? How does it work, in Spain?"

"Policia Nacional."

Petra nodded. "Well, it was them who fucked up, then. Not you. Don't let anyone convince you otherwise." She downed her second glass then put her hand over it when Susannah picked up the bottle of wine. "Not yet. My body needs time to catch up."

"If you need support, we have trauma counsellors," Susannah said. "I know it feels a bit like taking coals to Newcastle, but..."

"It doesn't. It can help to speak to someone you don't know. Even if you don't think you need to."

"I'll send you a name," Susannah said.

"Thanks," Petra replied. She took a deep, slow breath: in, out. "And there's something else I need from you."

"Name it."

Petra jerked her head upwards. "My case is packed, but I've missed the last flight to Heathrow."

"You're not going back to Glasgow?"

Petra felt her chest tighten. Could she confide in Susannah, tell her at least a little of the memories that awaited her in Glasgow?

No. Not yet.

"Heathrow," she said. "I've got a friend in London who I haven't visited for a while."

"Have we booked you a flight?"

"You have." Petra tapped her fingers on the table. "But this isn't about the flight. It's about the hotel room."

Susannah's face fell. "Oh, shit. God, I'm so sorry, Petra. You shouldn't have to go back up there."

"I'd rather not."

"And I should have invited you for a drink somewhere else."

Petra shrugged. "I've never set foot in this bar before tonight. You're fine."

"But you need me to organise you an alternative hotel."

"Please. I know it's an imposition, at nine thirty at night. But..."

Susannah gripped her shoulder. "It's not. I should have thought of it earlier. But at this time of night, with the office closed..."

Petra looked at her. *Surely you've got an expense card?*

Susannah gazed at her drink. "I'm in a rental apartment. There's a spare room."

Petra hadn't been expecting that. "Oh. I didn't..." Truth was, she needed to be alone. But she'd put Susannah on the spot. "Is there a cat?"

Susannah gave her a quizzical look. "A cat? In a rental apartment?"

"My ex-girlfriend had one. I'm beginning to realise I might have been allergic. If not to the fur, then to the cunning little bastards and the way they look at you."

Susannah laughed. "No," she said. "I don't have a cat. Neither here in Madrid, nor at home in Paris." She met Petra's gaze. "And nor did any of my ex-girlfriends."

Petra resisted a smile. So Susannah *had* been flirting with her.

And the Interpol agent was hot. Well out of Petra's

league, if anyone had asked her. Tall – surely too tall for Petra – with mid-brown skin, a trendy chopped haircut, and the tiniest glint of yellow in those eyes.

Far too hot for a five-foot-nothing Scotswoman with a history of fucking up relationships.

Petra reached for the bottle. She poured another glass of wine.

"The offer is very kind," she said. "But I really need some time alone right now."

Susannah's cheeks had reddened. "I understand," she said.

Petra looked at her over her glass. "You do?" she asked. "I haven't offended you?"

Susannah smiled. "Of course you haven't. Hell, after the day you've had..." She leaned in, the sparks of yellow becoming clearer. "You were amazing today. I should have said so earlier. The way you turned his words against him." She raised her glass.

Petra clinked hers against it. Bloody hell, had they finished the bottle already?

"Thank you," she said. "I appreciate that."

"And so do I," Susannah replied. "The presence of mind you showed. The understanding of how Morales was thinking." She licked her lips, making them glisten. "Let's just say I imagine I'll be hiring you again."

"I'd enjoy that," Petra said, surprising herself.

"Even after this afternoon?"

Petra regarded Susannah. Sure, today had been stressful. Terrifying, at times. But some things could be made worthwhile.

"Even after this afternoon," she said. "I hope we're able to work together again."

Thank you for reading *Veil of Blood*. I hope you enjoyed reading Susannah and Petra's first case as much as I enjoyed writing it.

Their next case is a full-length novel set in Paris, with the first clue found in the Louvre. It publishes in ebook and audiobook, as well as in a gorgeous hardback edition. To find out more and order your copy go to rachelmclean.com/paris

Happy reading!
Rachel

AUTHOR'S NOTE
HOW WELL DO YOU KNOW DR PETRA MCBRIDE?

Does Dr Petra McBride seem familiar to you?

If she does, that's because she has featured in almost all of my police procedural series to date.

In the Zoe Finch 'Deadly' books she appeared as an expert to help out with a spate of hate crimes in *Deadly Desires*, where her role was to help West Midlands Police identify the kind of person that would have committed those crimes.

In the Dorset Crime series, Lesley regularly consults her when she's trying to puzzle out what actually happened to DCI Mackie. When Lesley is given Mackie's suicide note, she asks Petra to analyse it and tell her if she believes the note was genuinely written by Mackie, or if it's a fake. Petra's insights, into the note and into Mackie's state of mind at his death, help Lesley to finally establish how Mackie died.

And then Petra got her own series. In my Scottish McBride & Tanner series, I decided to indulge myself. I thoroughly enjoyed writing Petra, so why not give her a starring role? She's brought in as an active consultant on all of the murders investigated by Police Scotland's fictional Complex Crimes Unit. She helps DI Jade Tanner out professionally and also offers her personal support in dealing with the death of her husband Dan. And she faces demons of her own – does she have a stalker? And if so, is it related to a past case?

While I was writing Petra into the McBride & Tanner series, I realised I was missing an opportunity.

Between books, Petra would go off on other cases she was hired to consult on as a forensic psychologist. And most of these cases were international.

So I thought, why not give her a new series set in international locations? That way both she and I could enjoy the challenge of getting to grips with policing in other countries as well as solving some very knotty crimes and brining some extremely unpleasant criminals to justice.

The Roscoe & McBride series is what resulted. It kicks off in Paris with *Veil of Secrets*, and will continue in European destinations including Barcelona, Prague and Rome. I can't wait to see what Petra gets up to next, and how her relationship with Interpol agent Susannah Roscoe develops.

Happy reading!
Rachel.

ALSO BY RACHEL MCLEAN

The DI Zoe Finch Series – buy from book retailers.

Deadly Wishes

Deadly Choices

Deadly Desires

Deadly Terror

Deadly Reprisal

Deadly Fallout

Deadly Christmas

The McBride & Tanner Series – buy from book retailers.

Blood and Money

Death and Poetry

Power and Treachery

Secrets and History

The Cumbria Crime Series by Rachel McLean and Joel Hames – buy from book retailers.

The Harbour

The Mine

The Cairn

The Barn

The Lake

The Wood

The Port

The Marsh

The Dorset Crime Series – buy from book retailers.

The Corfe Castle Murders

The Clifftop Murders

The Island Murders

The Monument Murders

The Millionaire Murders

The Fossil Beach Murders

The Blue Pool Murders

The Lighthouse Murders

The Ghost Village Murders

The Poole Harbour Murders

The Chesil Beach Murders

The Beach Hut Murders

...and more to come

Read the London Cosy Mystery Series by Rachel McLean and Millie Ravensworth – buy from book retailers.

Death at Westminster

Death in the West End

Death at Tower Bridge

Death on the Thames

Death at St Paul's Cathedral

Death at Abbey Road

The Jurassic Coast Mystery Series by Rachel McLean and Millie Ravensworth – buy from book retailers.

The Swimming Club

The Empty Easel

The Shattered Bauble

Printed and bound by CPI Group (UK) Ltd, Croydon, CR0 4YY

26/11/2025

02006146-0001